ANOTHER ULTIMATE YO-Y BOOK

More Great Tricks and Tips!

By Larry Sayco
Illustrated by Brian Floca

For my mother and father,
Mr. and Mrs. Louis and Alma Sayegh:
They put a lot more into life than what they got from it—L.S.

 Published by Grosset & Dunlap, a division of
Penguin Putnam Books for Young Readers, New York. GROSSET & DUNLAP
is a trademark of Grosset & Dunlap, Inc.
Published simultaneously in Canada. Printed in the U.S.A.
Library of Congress Catalog Card Number: 99-76111
ISBN 0-448-41968-8 A B C D E F G H I J

Table of Contents

Follow-Up and Down

As some of you may know, this is my second book for beginners on the Art of Spinning a Yo-Yo. The first, titled **The Ultimate Yo-Yo Book**, has many important and useful tips. If you still have your copy, you may want to review it before trying some of the more difficult maneuvers in this edition. Nevertheless, I have repeated some of the more important points, as well as the basic three tricks for those of you who are just getting started.

Single and Double Axle Loops

Inside the groove of a yo-yo, the string is looped around the axle. The string can be either single looped or double looped around the axle. Beginners sometimes find it easier to learn on a yo-yo that is double looped, but they soon have to switch over to a single loop. You can't do any of the sleeper tricks with the yo-yo double looped.

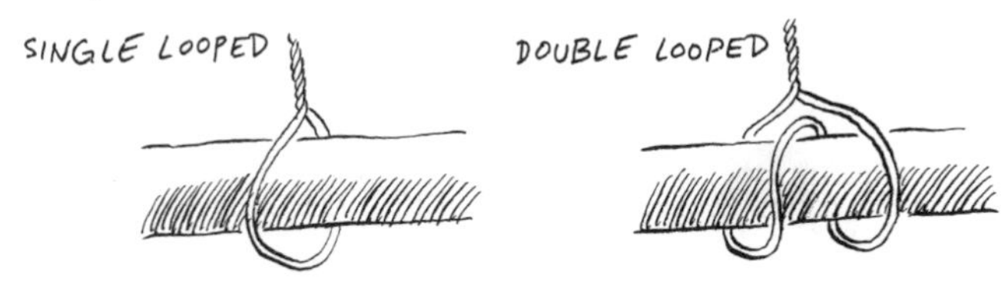

If your yo-yo is double looped, hold the string tightly and untwist the yo-yo to the left (counter clockwise) until you see two separate strings. Open the space between the strings and pass the yo-yo through it. Now your yo-yo is single looped. You may have to tighten the string by twisting the yo-yo to the right (clockwise).

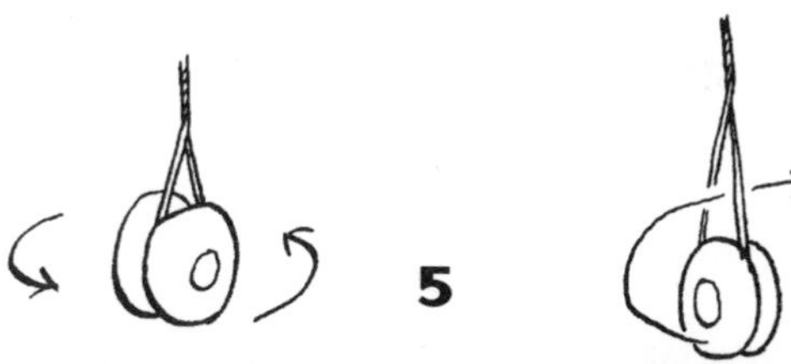

Helpful Hints to Get You Go-Going

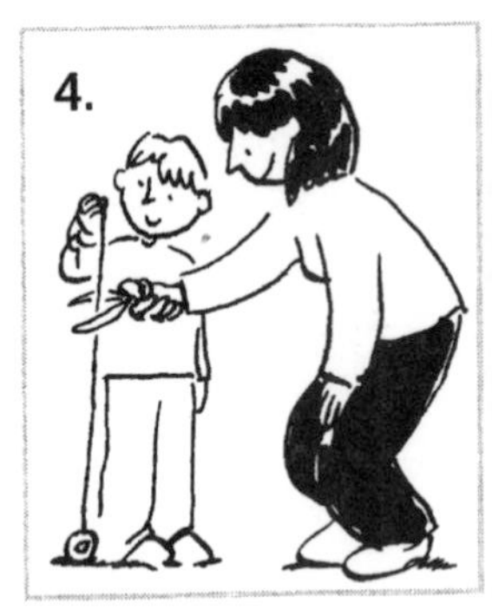

1. Make sure your yo-yo isn't too light. Use one that weighs at least an ounce.

2. Use a plain, old-fashioned yo-yo with a replaceable string. Any yo-yo that costs more than $3.00 — with a fancy name or a high-tech claim — won't improve your skill, and may distract you because of the adjustments, lubrication, battery replacement, polishing, and maintenance needed to keep it in top condition.

3. Don't take your yo-yo apart (unless it's a special yo-yo made to be taken apart).

4. Unwind the string and stand the yo-yo on the floor in front of you. Then have a grown-up cut the string even with your chest. The string will be a little long, but when you tie a finger loop, it should be just right — at your bellybutton.

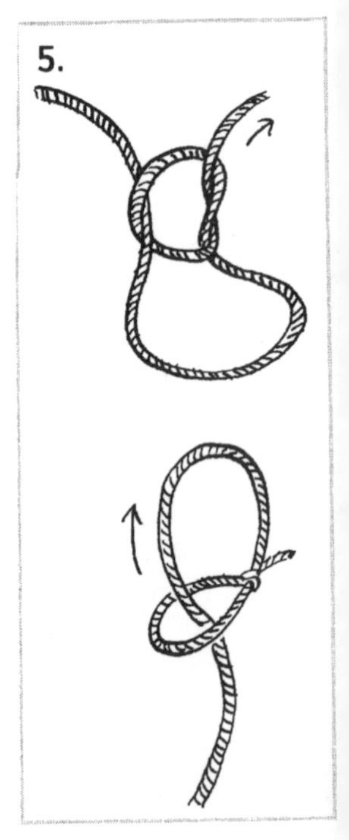

5. Tie a small loop at the end of the string, and pull part of the string through the loop each time you yo-yo for an easy slipknot.

6. Place the slipknot loop on your middle finger. Beginners should put the loop right next to their hand. Better players should keep the loop between the first and second knuckle.

7. A slipknot fits tightly over your finger while you are playing, but opens up easily when you want to take it off. If the string hurts or stops your blood flow, take a break for a while. Or lightly wrap a Band-Aid around your finger and put the loop over the Band-Aid.

8. Read all the directions for a trick before you try to do it.

9. Do each trick one step at a time. You can't do the hard tricks until you learn the easy ones.

10. Last but not least, always BE CAREFUL when using a yo-yo, even if you're alone. If you're doing the tricks in front of other people, make sure they know to stand back!

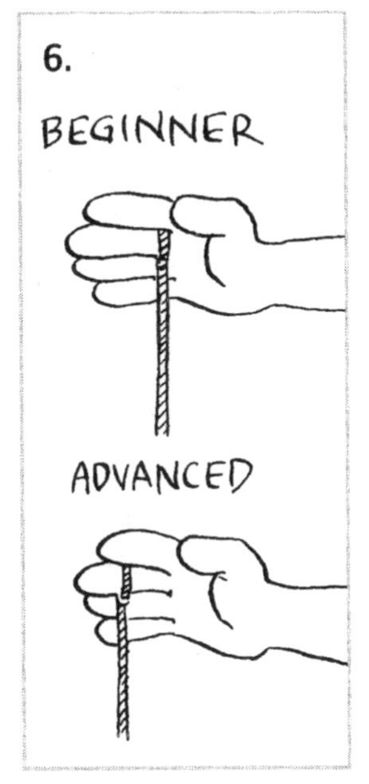

Don't Go Knots!

All yo-yo players, from beginners to pros, have trouble with knots. Here are some tips that may help:

Stop immediately as soon as you detect a knot. If the knot is in the yo-yo, use a straightened paper clip or even a stiff toothpick to pick it open. (Ask an adult to help.)

Never try to undo the knot with a knife.

If the knot is only in the length of the string, look closely at it to see how it's knotted. Then slowly try to pick it open.

Don't swing, pull, or dangle the yo-yo because you will only make the knot worse. Above all, have patience! You'll get it out if you follow the directions above and are careful.

Kinks

When the yo-yo string twists too tight, it will form tiny beads known as "kinks" or "pig-tailing." When this happens, let the yo-yo drop to the end of the string and it will automatically untwist itself.

Tip: When you buy a new yo-yo, pick up some extra string, preferably of the same brand. If your string breaks, wears out, or knots so badly that you have to cut it, the extra string will come in handy. Replace the string by following the manufacturer's instructions, which are usually printed on the yo-yo package.

A Review: Down and Up

1. Hold the yo-yo in your hand like a ball. Your palm should be down and about even with your bellybutton, but not touching your body.

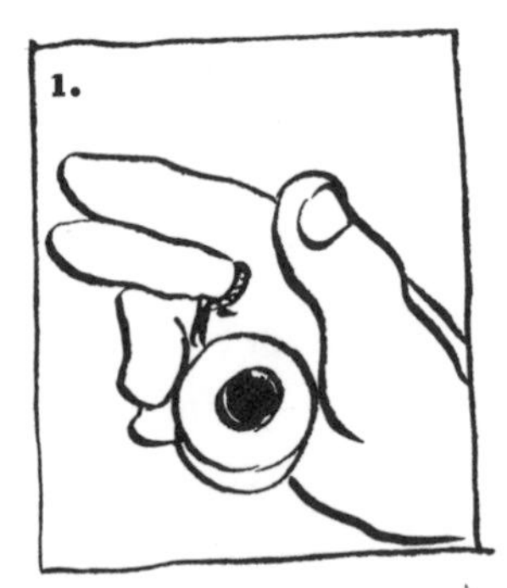

2. Open your hand and let the yo-yo drop toward the floor. As soon as you open your hand, say "yo-yo."

3. After the second "yo," smoothly lift your yo-yo hand up about 3 or 4 inches. You'll feel a snap when the yo-yo reaches the bottom of the string, and because of your tug, the yo-yo will climb up the opposite side of the string.

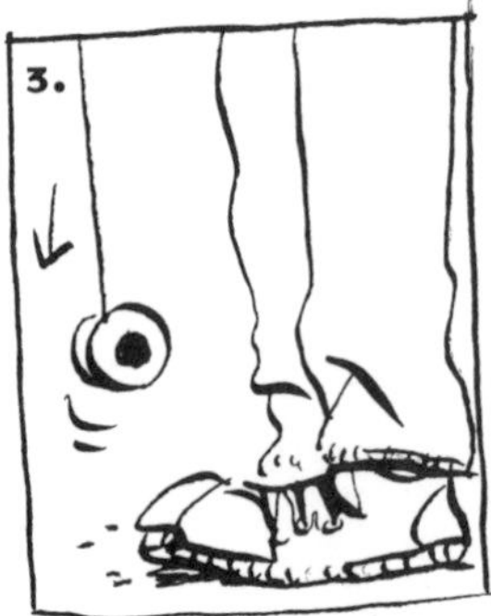

4. When the yo-yo reaches the top of the string, close your hand quickly to catch it.

Down and Up Trouble Tips

PROBLEM	CAUSE	WHAT TO DO
Yo-yo wobbles sideways.	Yo-yo isn't heavy enough.	Until you get a heavier one, tape a penny to the center of each side of the yo-yo.
Yo-yo keeps going sideways, and it's not the weight of the yo-yo.	You're pushing the yo-yo down when you open your hand.	Open your hand gently but quickly to let the yo-yo fall to Mother Earth.
Yo-yo goes down okay, but doesn't come up all the way, or doesn't come up at all.	Your tug timing is slightly off.	Instead of saying "yo-yo," try counting "one, two." Open on "one" and pull up on "two."
Yo-yo returns to your hand, but with a handful of spaghetti (unwound string).	You're grabbing the yo-yo too soon.	Wait until the yo-yo touches your hand before you snap it shut.

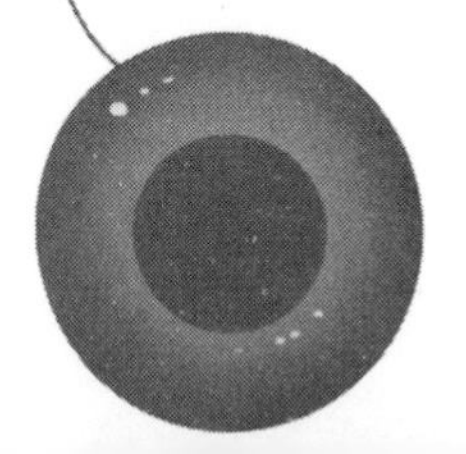

The Forward Pass

Practice this trick without the yo-yo a couple of times to get the feel of it.

1. Pretend you are about to throw a bowling ball. If you're right-handed, stand with your right foot slightly out in front. If you're left-handed, stand with your left foot slightly out in front.

2. Put your yo-yo hand, palm up, as far back as you can. Keep your wrist curled.

3. Swing your arm forward, uncurling your wrist. Let go of the yo-yo when your hand is even with your forward toe. This will send the yo-yo in front of you at an angle.

4. Once the yo-yo is completely out of your hand, turn your hand so your palm faces the ceiling again.

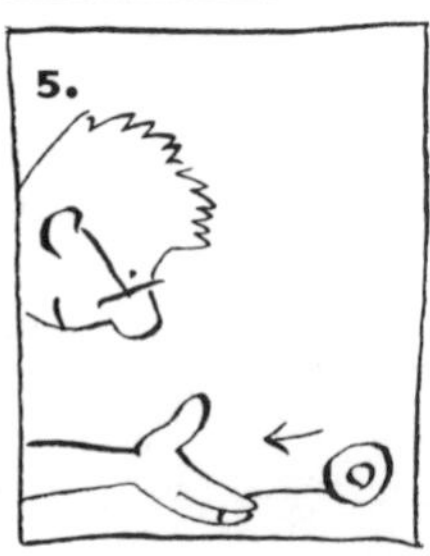

5. The yo-yo will spin to the end of the string, reverse itself, and return to your hand, where you can catch it.

Forward Pass Trouble Tips

PROBLEM	CAUSE	WHAT TO DO
Yo-yo twists when it leaves your hand.	You're twisting your hand too soon.	Make sure the yo-yo is completely out of your hand before the twist. Try counting again. Throw on "one," and twist on "two."
You can't catch the yo-yo on its return.	You're throwing either too hard or too soft.	A fast throw can be tough to catch. A soft throw won't make it all the way back. Adjust the speed of your throw.
Yo-yo goes out straight, but returns too high to catch.	You're releasing the yo-yo too late.	Remember to let go of the yo-yo when your hand passes your forward toe.

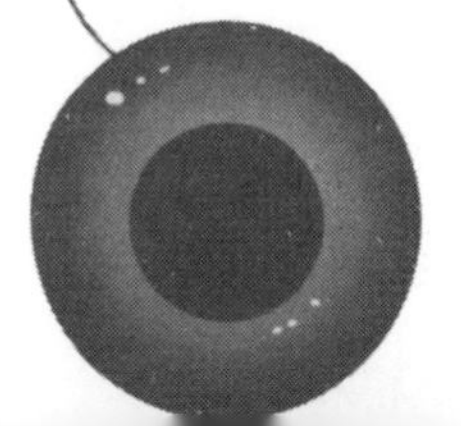

See how many Forward Passes in a row you can throw!

IMPORTANT NOTE! Before doing any tricks that include Sleepers, make sure your yo-yo is single looped (see page 5). Try a few simple tricks with the yo-yo single looped to get used to the feel of it before going on.

The Sleeper

1. Curl your hand, bend your elbow, and make a muscle like Popeye, but with your arm in front of you.

2. Give your hand, fingers, wrist, and arm a downward whipping motion—like you're shaking water off your hand—throwing the yo-yo out and in front of you.

3. As you throw the yo-yo, lift your hand 3 or 4 inches, then turn it so the palm faces the ground. If you do this right, the yo-yo will spin or "sleep" at the bottom of the string.

4. Give the string a quick upward tug to make the yo-yo return to you.

5. Catch it.

Sleeper Trouble Tips

PROBLEM	CAUSE	WHAT TO DO
Yo-yo sleeps but won't come back.	String is too loose.	Tighten by unwinding the yo-yo, then twisting it to the right (clockwise) about 20 times.
Yo-yo won't sleep. It returns as soon as you throw it.	String is too tight.	Loosen string by unwinding the yo-yo and letting it untwist to the left (counter clockwise).
	............**OR**.............	....
	You're throwing the yo-yo wrong.	Throw the yo-yo out and just leave it there. Don't tug or jerk the string at all.
Yo-yo slants to one side.	You're turning your hand too soon.	Make sure the yo-yo is completely out of your hand before you turn it.
	............**OR**.............	....
	Yo-yo isn't spinning fast enough.	Try throwing harder with more of a snap.
	............**OR**............	....
	You're slanting the throw.	Practice in a room with straight lines on the floor. Stand with your feet parallel to the lines. Then throw the yo-yo so that it spins parallel to those lines.

Blo-Yo

1. Start by throwing a Sleeper.

2. While the yo-yo is spinning, raise your hand as high as you can to get the yo-yo about 12 inches away from your face.

3. Look straight at the yo-yo. Take a big breath and then puff hard at the yo-yo while flicking your yo-yo finger with your thumb. This will make the yo-yo return to your hand and make your friends think you just blew it back up.

Blo-Yo Trouble Tips

PROBLEM	CAUSE	WHAT TO DO
Yo-yo sleeps but comes up when you raise your hand.	String is too tight.	Loosen the string a little to the left.
	............OR.............	....
	Lifting is too jerky.	Lift hand smoothly in one quick motion.
Yo-yo spins but won't return on the flick.	String is too loose.	Twist to the right to tighten string.
	............OR.............	....
	Yo-yo string loop is placed too far back on finger.	Put the finger loop up closer to the first knuckle of your yo-yo finger.
	............OR.............	....
	Sleeper is too slow.	Throw a faster Sleeper.

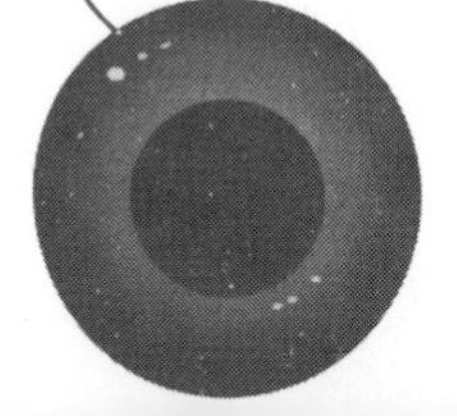

Yo-Yo Catch

1. Throw a fast Sleeper.

2. Raise your yo-yo hand high enough to place the palm of your free hand directly under the spinning yo-yo.

3. Count to three, and on "three," stop, catch, and hold on to the yo-yo in one quick motion.

PROBLEM	CAUSE	WHAT TO DO
Yo-yo rolls away from you too fast for you to hold on to it.	Grabbing the yo-yo upwards.	Close fingers quickly around yo-yo without moving your palm up.

Some of your friends will think this is really simple. Let them try and see if they can catch it. Remember, only one try — and no fumbling around with your free hand.

Efaham and Goofus

1. Do a Forward Pass.

2. As the yo-yo returns, when it's about 12 to 15 inches away, put your free hand out and catch it without any help from your yo-yo hand or the rest of your body.

Sounds easy enough, doesn't it? Try it a few times before reading the solution below.

What to Do: Don't catch the yo-yo palm up. The catch must be made with the palm of your free hand facing out so you can see the back of your free hand. As the yo-yo returns, make the string go in between the fingers of your free hand. Once you catch it, you should have 6 to 12 inches of slack string between both hands.

Practice this trick so that when you challenge your friends it will look so easy they might laugh — until they try it themselves.

Okee Funokee

1. Hold the yo-yo in front of you at around the height of your chest but about 10 inches away so you can see the back of your yo-yo hand.

2. Slowly and gently lift your yo-yo hand up with a snap and release the yo-yo, so it will climb straight up about 2 to 6 inches, maximum.

3. As the yo-yo comes down, guide it with a circular motion of your wrist and send it forward in front of you. It will go to the end of the string and then return to you. Catch it underhand.

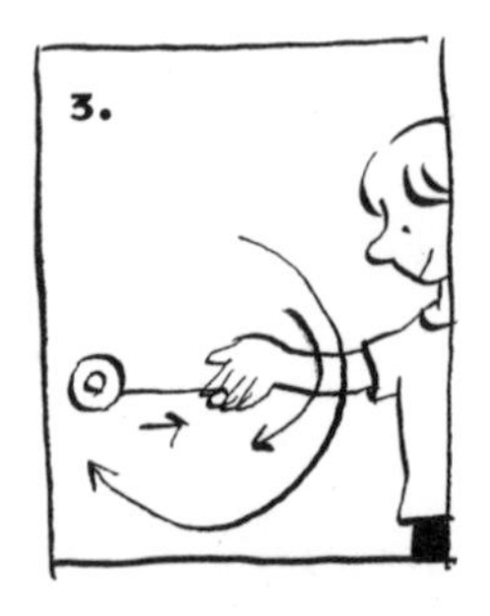

Okee Funokee Trouble Tips

PROBLEM	CAUSE	WHAT TO DO
You lose control of the yo-yo as you throw it up.	Your throw is too hard.	Just barely let the yo-yo out of your hand.
When the yo-yo comes down, you can't swing it back out.	Your snap is too weak.	Snap your wrist hard.
	............OR.............	....
	Your timing is off.	Practice a few snaps late, then a few early, then try to close the gap between them.

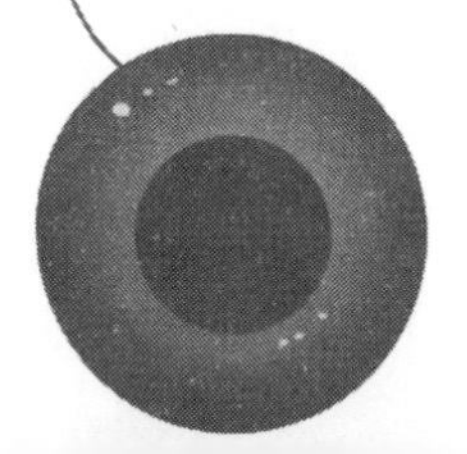

The Backward Dog Walk

1. Start by doing the Around the World trick, which goes like this: Begin with a Forward Pass, but swing your arm a little higher in front of you, stopping when your hand is about level with your shoulder. (Don't turn your hand as you usually would for a Forward Pass.) The yo-yo should move up and back, making a large circle outside your arm. When the yo-yo completes a circle, turn your hand around and give the yo-yo a tug to wake it up, then catch it underhand.

2. Now, instead, as the yo-yo swings around and passes your leg, put your yo-yo hand over the yo-yo to bring its swinging motion to a dead stop.

3. Lower your hand gently to the floor, guiding the yo-yo as it walks backward toward you.

Backward Dog Walk Trouble Tips

PROBLEM	CAUSE	WHAT TO DO
Yo-yo won't stop swinging.	You're using too much arm muscle.	When you start, use more of your wrist and hand instead.
Yo-yo doesn't spin long enough.	You're throwing it wrong.	Curl your wrist, and then open it with a sudden snap.
Yo-yo comes up as soon as it touches the floor.	Your touchdown is too hard.	As you lower your hand, let the yo-yo just lightly skim the floor surface.
	...........OR...........	....
	The string is at an angle when the yo-yo touches the floor.	Keep the string straight; the yo-yo should not swing during the touchdown.

Practice this trick outside first, until you have good control. Don't overthrow the yo-yo; use just enough force as necessary to complete the trick.

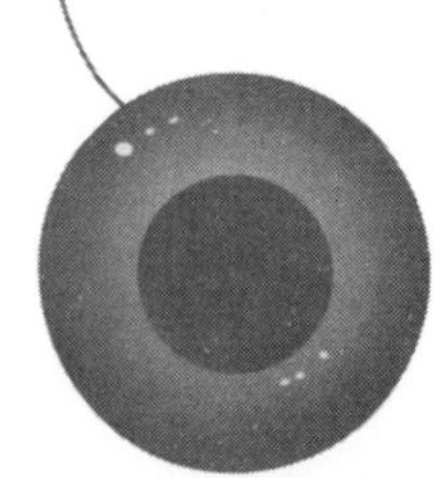

Tip: Use a board or something smooth to walk your yo-yo on outside, so you won't scuff up its edges.

Otis's Elevator

1. Throw a fast Sleeper.

2. With the index finger of your free hand, touch the string at the front next to your yo-yo finger and pull up about 2 inches. Now, with your yo-yo hand, make a loose fist around both strands of string and pull it back, with your index finger towards you, approximately 3 inches. Stop and announce, "First Floor!" Then go back another 3 inches and repeat, announcing, "Second Floor!" Go back another 3 inches and repeat for "Third Floor!"

3. Move your free hand toward your fist to let the yo-yo come down one floor at a time. Or, if your spin isn't hard enough, go right down to the basement. Then bring it up and catch it.

Otis's Elevator Trouble Tips

PROBLEM	CAUSE	WHAT TO DO
The string burns your finger, making it difficult to pull up.	The string or your hands are wet.	Dry your hands really well, or put a little talcum powder on that part of your finger.
	............OR............	....
	You're sandwiching the string between your thumb and index finger.	Use only the index finger to pull up.
	............OR............	....
	You're squeezing your fist too tight.	Relax your grip.
The yo-yo won't keep spinning.	You're throwing the sleeper sideways, increasing the friction on the string.	Throw a harder and straighter sleeper.
	............OR............	....
	You're taking too long to do the trick.	Until you know it well, don't stop on each floor — just practice going up and down.

Tip: Don't be too anxious to get the yo-yo back. If it's spinning too fast when you catch it, you'll end up with a handful of tangled spaghetti.

Skin the Cat

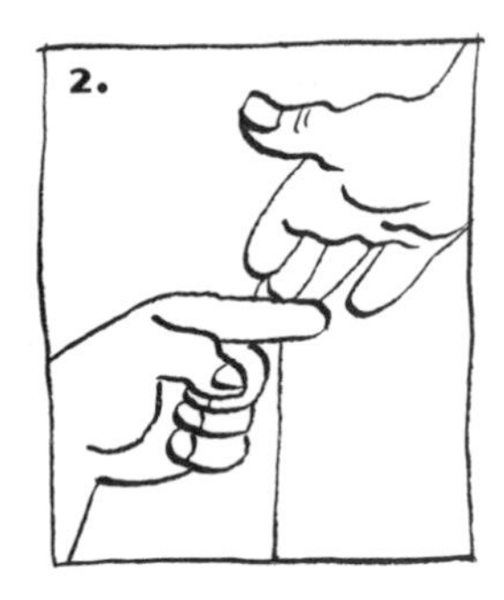

1. Start by throwing a Sleeper.

2. Point the index finger of your free hand toward your yo-yo hand and touch your middle finger underneath, but in back of the yo-yo string.

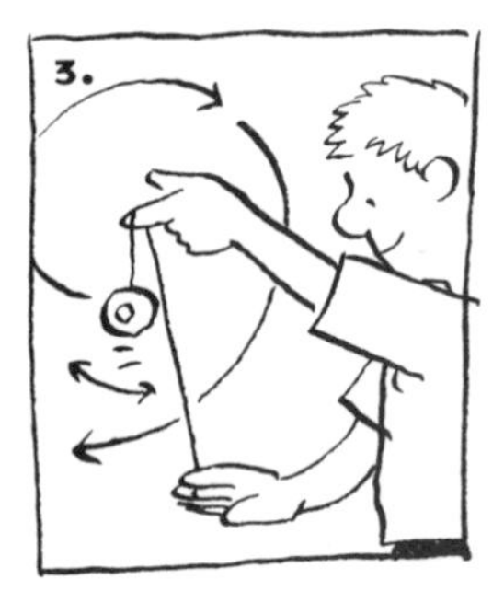

3. Push your free hand up and forward to about 6 inches away from the yo-yo, making it swing back and forth. Then toss the yo-yo upward, pulling your index finger out of the way.

4. Gravity and force will pull the yo-yo back down toward your yo-yo hand, but don't catch it. Just snap your wrist in a circular motion as if doing a loop.

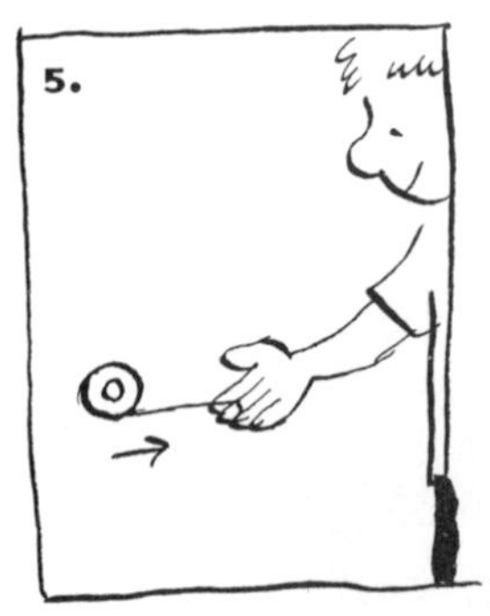

5. The yo-yo will then go straight out in front of you and return to your hand for an underhand catch.

Skin The Cat Trouble Tips

PROBLEM	CAUSE	WHAT TO DO
When I toss the yo-yo up, it won't come back.	String is too loose.	Check and tighten by spinning the yo-yo to the right (clockwise).
When I toss the yo-yo up, it comes back too suddenly or it's crooked.	String is too tight. ....OR............ Rough or choppy swing.	Check and loosen by spinning the yo-yo to the left. .... Gently swing yo-yo back and up toward yourself.
When the yo-yo loops out, I can't make the catch.	You're catching overhand. ....OR............ The yo-yo is moving too fast.	Make the catch underhand. .... Use more time doing the trick to let the spin slow down.

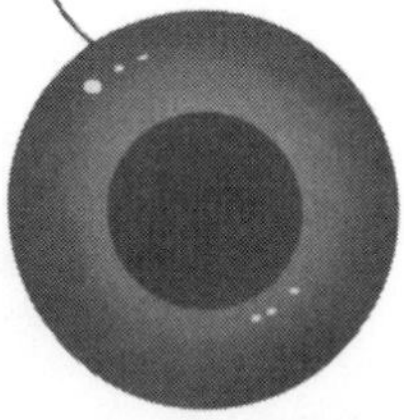

Tip: It's best to keep your yo-yo hand no higher than your waist once the yo-yo is spinning.

Alley Oop

1. Throw a fast Sleeper.

2. With the index finger of your free hand, touch the middle finger of your yo-yo hand in front of the yo-yo string.

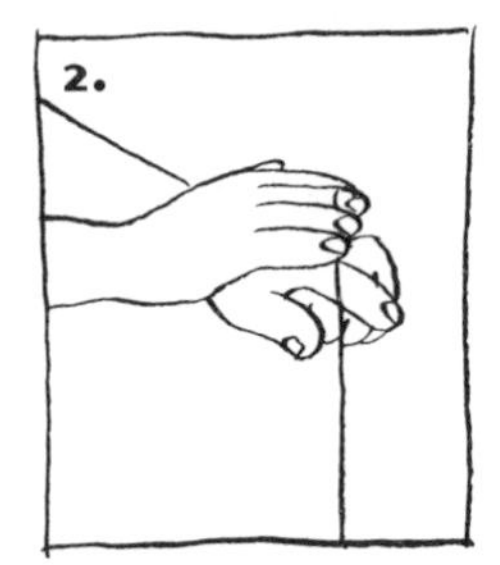

3. Push your index finger straight up to about 2 inches from the yo-yo, then pinch the string, keeping your yo-yo hand about even with your waist and the yo-yo almost straight above your shoulder.

4. Keeping your head up, look at the spinning yo-yo. Release the pinch; the yo-yo will quickly drop to your yo-yo hand. Be ready to snap your wrist and shoot it back out in front of you by looping it out and catching it when it returns to your hand.

Although similar to Skin the Cat, this trick is more difficult because you catch the string on the opposite side of your finger. When you practice, wait until the spin slows down quite a bit before you release the pinch on top.

Show Tip: If you're performing this on stage, as you bring your finger up try arching your back (like you're doing the limbo), then release the pinch. Loop, then catch.

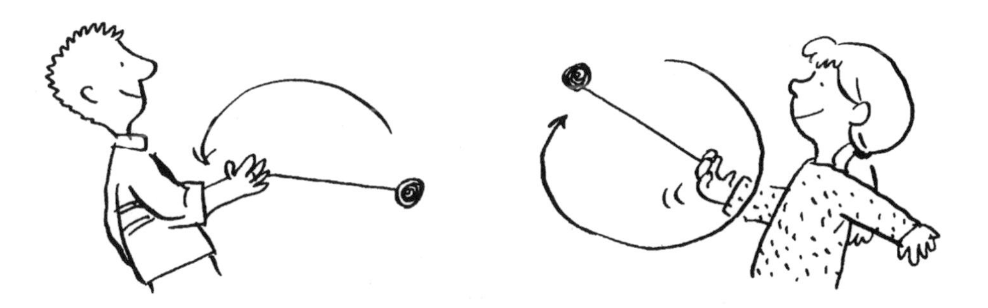

Hanky Panky

1. Open up a plain, clean handkerchief and spread it on a table or chair.

2. With your thumb and middle finger, pick up the handkerchief in the center and stuff it into your side pants or coat pocket on your yo-yo side. Push it in about halfway and let the rest hang out.

3. Throw the yo-yo down hard and close enough so the string almost touches the handkerchief on the way down. On the way back up, it will grab the hanky and pull it completely out of your pocket. Wave it to your audience, or pretend you just sneezed and needed a handkerchief to blow your nose.

Hanky Panky Trouble Tips

PROBLEM	CAUSE	WHAT TO DO
Spectacular trick! But now how do I separate them afterward?	You're throwing too hard.	Try a softer throw, then gently pull them apart. ....OR..................... Unwind the string one turn at a time from the yo-yo.
Yo-yo won't pull hanky all the way out, or it partly comes out and falls to the ground	You're throwing the yo-yo wrong. ....OR............ There's too much hanky material protruding from your pocket.	Practice throwing both slow and fast until you get the right amount of speed needed. .... Pull out just one corner at a time so there's less for the yo-yo to grab.

Show Tip: Sew one corner of a small flag to the center of the hanky. Make sure the flag does not show on the part of the hanky that's hanging out. If you do this right, the flag will appear and be greeted with applause, which you can lead with your own "Ta-daa!"

Yo-Ball

1. Crumple up a sheet of paper into a ball.

2. Throw it into the air, and as it comes down try to hit it with a Forward Pass.

3. Keep your mind on the yo-yo so you can catch it when it returns, whether you hit the Yo-Ball or not.

PROBLEM	CAUSE	WHAT TO DO
You can't throw it very far or the wind takes it.	The Yo-Ball is too light.	Use a bigger piece of paper (like newspaper) and pack it tight and small.
Trouble hitting the ball.	Your timing is off, or you're just lobbing it.	Throw the Yo-Ball high enough to give you more time to get ready . . . aim . . . and strike!

Strike Out!

This trick is similar to Yo-Ball, except that you have a friend pitch the ball to you from about 12 feet away, trying to strike you out. If he does, it's your turn to pitch to him and try to strike him out. With practice, you can get almost the same control that you can swinging a bat.

More Fun!: You can even go a step further and apply basic baseball rules to make it a game. Start by deciding how far you have to hit the Yo-Ball to get an automatic first, second, third base, and home run hit. Use the same rules for flies, foul balls, strike outs, hitting the yo-yoer, and so forth. Before starting, decide how many innings you want to play and if you want slow underhand lobbing or fast overhand pitching. You won't even need a scoreboard; just play and enjoy! It helps to get a third person to be the catcher — otherwise, play with your back near a wall.

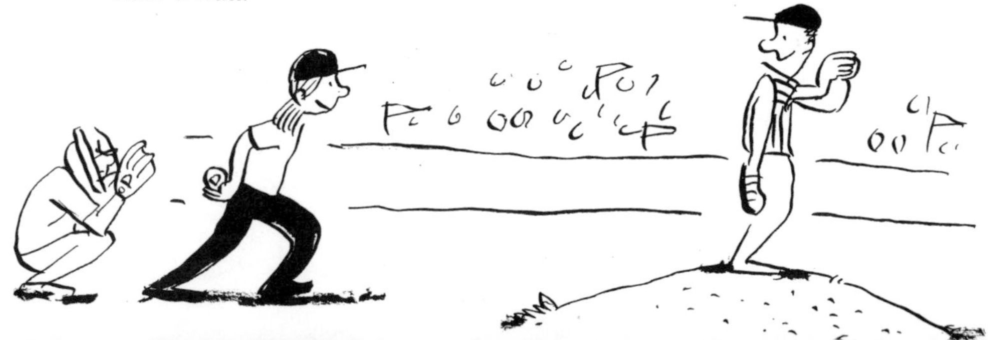

A Shoe-In

1. Place one plain shoe with a low top on a small table, chair, shelf, or anything that will elevate it to approximately half of your height.

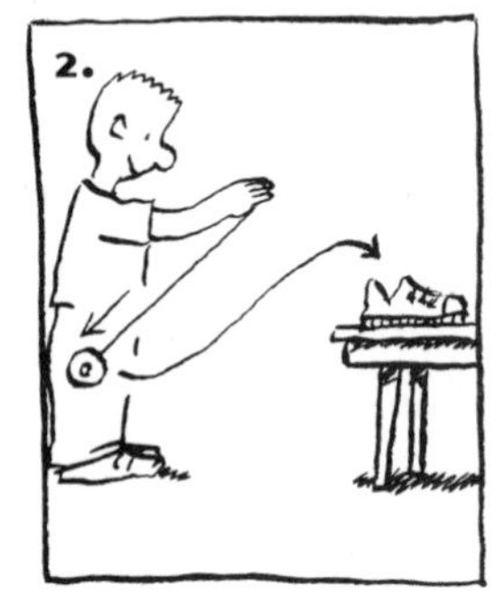

2. Stand 3 to 4 feet in front of it, facing the heel end. Throw a straight Sleeper to your side (not in front). This will make the yo-yo swing all the way back, and as it returns on the forward swing, guide it into the shoe — which is the easy part.

3. The hard part is pulling the spinning yo-yo out and catching it without moving the shoe.

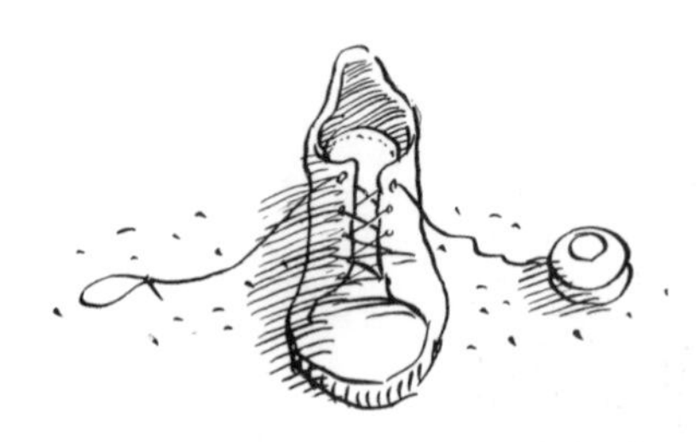

Shoe-In Trouble Tips

PROBLEM	CAUSE	WHAT TO DO
Yo-yo returns on the swing.	String is too tight.	Check and loosen to the left if needed.
The shoe moves too easily.	Shoe or slipper is too light.	Use a larger, adult-sized shoe, or stuff the toe end with something to weigh it down (like a bag of marbles).
The yo-yo stops when it lands in the shoe.	Your hand is too low on the upswing.	Raise your yo-yo hand high when swinging it in, and even higher when pulling it up and out.
You can't make the catch when the yo-yo returns.	You're catching or grabbing overhand.	Use underhand catch (palm up). This is hard to do with your hand up high, so keep practicing!

Yo First Pocket Trick

1. For this trick you need a shirt with a pocket, preferably on your yo-yo side. If it is buttoned, unbutton the flap and tuck it into the pocket. If it is pressed closed, open it and make sure the yo-yo fits easily inside.

2. With your free hand, hold your pocket open. Slowly do a Forward Pass as if you want to do a Loop, keeping your yo-yo hand at the same height as your pocket.

3. As the yo-yo returns, instead of curling your wrist fully to do a complete circle, curl it only halfway, guiding the string on your middle finger directly into your open pocket.

4. As you practice you'll find you can do this trick without having to hold your pocket open. With more practice, you can end a routine by doing Loops and letting the final one flop into your pocket.

Pocket Trick Trouble Tips

PROBLEM	CAUSE	WHAT TO DO
Yo-yo doesn't return.	String is too loose.	Check and tighten to the right.
	...........OR............	....
	You're throwing in an arc.	Throw yo-yo straight out.
	...........OR............	....
	You're throwing too gently.	Increase force a little at a time.
On the return, the yo-yo misses and loops out and away from the pocket.	Your yo-yo hand is too far from your pocket.	On the return, bring your yo-yo hand closer and above the pocket to let the yo-yo dunk in.

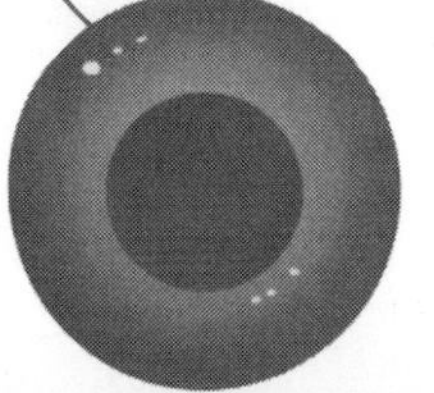

Winding Like the Pros

Note: *The following is an important timesaving instructional trick. Master it now before you move on to more difficult tricks.*

1. Unwind the yo-yo and put it in your other hand. Place your thumb over the groove where the string comes out. Hold the yo-yo steady with the index and middle fingers of your other hand, below the yo-yo. Put your yo-yo hand high above your other hand, which should give your string approximately a 45-degree angle.

2. Push down the hand holding the yo-yo hard enough to make the yo-yo roll off the surface of your thumb. This will make the yo-yo climb the string partway. As the yo-yo goes back down, pull up before it reaches the bottom and it will climb up further.

3. Repeating this up and down move several times will eventually make the yo-yo return to your yo-yo hand.

Hot Tip #1: When practicing this maneuver for the first several times, double loop your string (see page 5). Once you get the hang of it, switch to the single loop and try it that way. Even though it's much harder, with practice you will soon be able to swish the yo-yo all the way back up in a second.

Hot Tip #2: Don't roll your thumb around the contour of the yo-yo when starting; keep it stiff and pointing toward the ceiling. Also, at the beginning, the yo-yo should touch the base of your thumb so it has more thumb surface off of which to roll.

Testing 1, 2, 3 . . .

Here is a simple exercise you can try yourself or have someone give to you.

1. Before starting, decide how many tricks you'll do and what they will be.

2. Don't ask anyone to give you the test unless they know a bit about yo-yos, but remember you must honor their decision no matter how much you disagree with it. Giving a test is easy. Giving a test and being *fair* is very difficult.

3. Add up the points for the tricks you selected in the following manner:

Good on the first try	=	10 points	**Platinum**
Good on the second try	=	7 points	**Gold**
Good on the third try	=	4 points	**Silver**
Missed on the third try	=	2 points	**Bronze**

Remember, by repeating this exercise over and over again, you will start to feel confident enough to do all these tricks in front of an audience — whether it's in a yo-yo contest or on stage.

Sample Score Sheet

TRICK	FIRST TRY (10 points)	SECOND TRY (7 points)	THIRD TRY (4 points)	MISSED ON THIRD TRY (2 points)	SCORE
Down and Up	✔				10
Forward Pass	✔				10
Sleeper	✔				10
Blo-Yo		✔			7
Otis's Elevator			✔		4
Okee Funokee	✔				10
Efaham and Goofus		✔			7
Hanky Panky				✔	2

Maximum Score for this Test: 80 points Total. . . . **60**

Judge: Ryan Wright Scorekeeper: Roberta Write

Note: The blank score sheet on the next page may be photocopied and scored in pencil for practice sessions. Good luck!

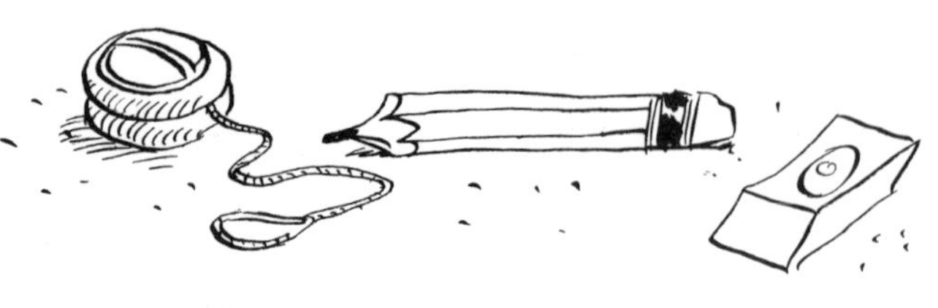

Blank Score Sheet

Name: Date:

TRICK	FIRST TRY (10 points)	SECOND TRY (7 points)	THIRD TRY (4 points)	MISSED ON THIRD TRY (2 points)	SCORE

Maximum Score for this Test: ______Points Point Total: _____

Judge: ______________________ Scorekeeper: ______________________

Yo-Yo Contest for Yo Buddies

Here are rules for a contest using as few or as many contestants as you wish. You can also use as few or as many tricks as you wish. Once you have all decided which tricks to use, you have to agree on who will be the judge — maybe the winner of the last contest, for instance.

The contestants line up side by side, preferably against a wall, house, or fence. Each person has three chances to complete the same trick — and if they don't, they are eliminated from the contest. If a contestant does the trick on the first, second, or third try, he or she stays in line for the next trick. Do the easiest tricks first, to get everyone warmed up. No practicing in between, except for adjusting string tension or simple Throw Downs and Sleepers.

When all the tricks are completed, the last person left is the winner. If there is more than one person left, each of them gets only one chance to do as many inside loops as they can without stopping. If they fail to catch the yo-yo on the last loop, that number still holds. Basically, you don't have to catch it; just keep looping until the string breaks or your finger falls off. No second chances on this one! The person who does the most loops is the winner.

If there is a tie, the top loopers should do battle again in the same manner until somebody comes out on top. Unexpected interference from an animal or another person justifies a repeat from scratch, unless the contestant wants to stick with that number. However, unexpected interference from a stationary object such as a pole, tree, or fire hydrant does not justify a looper to start over again.

Good luck, and have fun!

Tip: Don't waste your three chances! If you can't do a trick on your first or second try, stop and try to figure out what's wrong, so you can correct it before using up your last chance.

About the Author

The year 2001 marks an important anniversary for Larry Sayco. In September 1951, he accepted a job as a Yo-Yo Demonstrator "until better things came along." Fortunately, they never did, and he is still in the yo-yo business — traveling, entertaining, writing, and most especially making millions of his own unique yo-yos in his one-man "Top Shop" in Pawtucket, Rhode Island. Larry says: "If you love what you do, then stick to it, and if you don't get rich or famous, at least you'll be happy."

Official
YO-YO CHAMP
Award

We, the author and publisher of

Another Ultimate Yo-Yo Book

at the start of the third millennium
hereby recognize your outstanding
effort and practice in the world of yo-yos
and grant you,

____

Tethered-Top **"CHAMP-IN-TRAINING"** *Rank*
with the hope that your future endeavors
bring you everlasting
joy and peace.

Date __________

Publisher

Grosset & Dunlap

Author

[signature]